THE
MAGIC
DOOR

HOWARD FAST is a widely acclaimed writer of diverse talent who has written more than fifty books. He is best known as the celebrated author of *Freedom Road, Spartacus,* and the more recent trilogy of *The Immigrants, The Second Generation,* and *The Establishment. The Magic Door* gives the reader an unusual look into the time and conditions of Fast's own childhood in New York City. Fast once commented, "Books—especially fiction—are for the young; when they are good, they open a thousand doors." Howard Fast and his wife, Bette, live in Los Angeles.

THE MAGIC DOOR

BY HOWARD FAST
ILLUSTRATED BY BONNIE B. METTLER

Originally published as *TONY AND THE WONDERFUL DOOR*

AN AVON CAMELOT BOOK

This book was originally published in 1952 under the title
TONY AND THE WONDERFUL DOOR

AVON BOOKS
A division of
The Hearst Corporation
959 Eighth Avenue
New York, New York 10019

Copyright © 1979, 1968, 1952 by Howard Fast
Illustrations Copyright © 1979 by Bonnie B. Mettler
Published by arrangement with Peace Press
Library of Congress Catalog Card Number: 79-2578
ISBN: 0-380-51193-2

First Camelot Printing, October, 1980

The Peace Press edition carries the following Library of Congress
Cataloging in Publication Data:

   SUMMARY: When he has just the right feeling,
Tony can open the door in his New York City tenement
backyard and step through to the time when the
Dutch and Indians lived on Manhattan Island—but
no one believes him.
   [1. New York (City)—History—Colonial period,
ca. 1600-1775—Fiction.   2. Space and time—
Fiction]   I. Mettler, Bonnie.   II. Title.

CAMELOT TRADEMARK REG. U.S. PAT. OFF. AND IN
OTHER COUNTRIES, MARCA REGISTRADA, HECHO EN
U.S.A.

Printed in the U.S.A.

For Rachel and Jon

CONTENTS

THE MAGIC DOOR

1

Tony and the Teacher

"Why," asked Tony MacTavish Levy, "do you keep calling them wild? They are not wild. They are just nice, quiet people, like any other people."

"I see," said Miss Clatt, getting that look on her face. "In other words, Tony, you know more about Indians than I do."

It wasn't what she said but the way she said it that made the rest of the class laugh and look at Tony. Here would be one of those scenes again, and everyone was set to enjoy it except Tony. He stiffened in his chair, set his mouth grimly, and stared straight ahead of him.

"Well, Tony," said Miss Clatt, "do you know more about Indians than I do?"

"No . . ."

"But you were insolent enough to inform me that they were not wild—that they were just nice, quiet people, like any other people. So I'm sure you know more about Indians than I do, since you contradicted me so positively."

Tony MacTavish Levy was a thorn in Miss Clatt's side. Now she had a chance for revenge and she took it. Tony was already in deep, and Miss Clatt made up her mind that he would be in a good deal deeper before she allowed the matter to drop.

"I don't know more about Indians than you do, Miss Clatt," said Tony, very slowly and carefully, "I only know what I know about them."

"Which is all any of us could say," smiled Miss Clatt, fetching another wave of mocking laughter from the class. "But what you know seems to be a great deal, Tony. How do you know so much about the Indians?"

"I just know."

"Oh, I see," said Miss Clatt. "Perhaps you have some friends who are Indians, Tony?"

"I have," he said.

Miss Clatt quieted the laughter that ran through the class. Those of the students who knew both her and Tony MacTavish Levy sensed the crisis and settled themselves tensely to watch it approach.

"So you have friends who are Indians, Tony. A whole tribe, perhaps?"

"Just a village," said Tony.

"I see. And where is this Indian village, Tony?"

"Uptown," answered Tony, determinedly yet resignedly.

Miss Clatt's eyes narrowed. As she was fond of saying, she could tolerate all things in a child except lies. Also, she liked to make an example, caring less about how the child in question felt than about driving the question home.

"So there is an Indian village uptown, Tony, and you have friends there, and all this is happening in New York City in the year 1924. Just where is this Indian village, Tony, and who are the Indians who live there?"

"It takes about three hours to walk to the village," answered Tony, sadly but doggedly. "And the Indians are called the *Wesquaesteek*. They are not wild but very nice and gentle, and I don't care if you believe me."

"I cannot abide a liar," said Miss Clatt. "You will stay after school, Tony."

So Tony stayed after school. The worst part of it was that he knew he wouldn't be able to try the door today. That was worse than having to write on the blackboard, three hundred times, *I will tell no more lies.*

Then he was sent home with a letter to his father, which was worse than anything else.

His days in school almost amounted to a feud between Tony and Miss Clatt, because there was just about nothing at all on which they saw eye to eye. When they were separated from each other, they were entirely different from what they were

no more lies. I will tell no
no more lies. I
o more lies I
ANDERSON
MAINTAINING
DISCIPLINE
IN THE

together. Together, they spelled trouble for each other, and excitement for the rest of the class. Miss Clatt was a rather nice-looking woman, but to Tony, she was a teacher, which meant someone to be wary of. Tony was a short, snub-nosed, freckle-faced boy who had so few troubles in his life that he was in no way prepared to deal with Miss Clatt, who had many more. Otherwise they were fairly evenly matched.

It began the first day of class, the very first day, when Miss Clatt made herself—as she put it—familiar with the students' backgrounds. Miss Clatt had a social sense. Teaching in a school in New York's lower east side, she felt it was very important to become acquainted with the background of each of her pupils. That was her excuse for asking each of them the question about his or her national origin.

"I haven't any," said Tony, when his turn came, and that was the beginning of the first round between Tony MacTavish Levy and Miss Clatt.

"Everyone has a national origin," said Miss Clatt severely. She meant everyone in the class except herself. Miss Clatt never thought of herself as having a national origin. "Where did your parents come from?"

"My father came from Brooklyn," said Tony, which Miss Clatt was forced to consider more disruptive than informative. "My mother came from the state of Washington. Her name was MacTavish, but her mother was half Indian and half Swede. Her father was Scottish, except that his mother was Irish. And my grandmother, I mean my father's mother, is Italian and I'm named Tony after her father, only he was French from Marseilles, but his mother and father were Italian before they came to Marseilles where a lot of Italians go to live."

Without pausing for a breath, Tony said, "And my father's Jewish. I mean his father was and not my grandmother who was Italian but my grandfather was Russian and Lithuanian, except that he was Jewish, too—and that's why I haven't any."

"You haven't any what?" whispered Miss Clatt. The firm schoolroom floor under her feet had begun to feel like wet sand sucking her down.

"National origin," said Tony, "except my father came across the river from Brooklyn in 1912."

Miss Clatt let the matter drop right there. But that was the beginning of the ever-widening gap between Tony MacTavish Levy and herself, nor was that broad gap ever healed. Miss Clatt could never decide whether Tony was very stupid or very bright, very innocent or very cunning.

Tony lived on Mott Street, just a couple of blocks below Houston Street. Mott Street begins at Houston Street and runs south from there to the very end of Manhattan Island, and the southern end of the street is in Chinatown. Tony was very interested in Chinatown. Twice already he had walked down there with his father and mother and eaten a real family dinner with nine courses for only sixty cents, and until he discovered the door in his own back yard, he had considered Chinatown the most exciting place in the world.

The part of Mott Street where he lived, however, was a long way from Chinatown, and it consisted of a number of narrow old tenements of red brick, all the same and side by side.

Tony lived in one of these tenements, one flight up and in the rear. There, he and his father and mother shared a three room apartment. All three of the rooms were very small, but Tony's was the smallest of all. There he slept, and in the second room, which was just a little larger, his father and mother slept. In the third room, which was the kitchen, the three of them lived and ate and conducted all the business of being a family.

They were poor, but Tony was not conscious of that because everyone he knew was just as poor or even poorer. In other families, where there were three, four, five, and even ten children, no one ever had a room all to himself. But Tony was the only child in this family, and he had a room to himself. He also had a window to himself and outside the window, a fire escape to himself. He could go out the window and down the fire escape and be at the door in just about three minutes.

That is—not the door of the house, but the door of the back

yard fence. The tenement house in which Tony lived had a back yard, which was enclosed by a fence some ten feet high. In this fence, there was a little door. This door opened into the back yard of the tenement house on the next street, the house whose back wall faced the back wall of the house where Tony lived.

This was Tony's magic door. In order to get to it from his window, all Tony had to do was go out on the fire escape, climb down the ladder, and hang by his hands. Then he dropped onto an old bedspring. After he had bounced for a while, he stepped from there onto an old stove. Then he went around a big pile of tin cans, past a broken dresser and an ancient icebox. He avoided a hair mattress, took two steps on a rusty drain pipe, and climbed over a wagon seat. Only a sofa with stuffing and springs coming out of every corner of it remained to be passed before Tony was at the magic door.

All the way home, Tony debated the question of whether he should give Miss Clatt's letter to his father, or whether he should open it, read it, and then tear it into convenient little pieces. It was not that he was afraid of his father's reaction. His father had never licked him, but his father had a way of looking at him that hurt worse than a licking. He would look at Tony, and his look said, "Everything I do is for you, and now you've let me down." While Tony loved his father, he could not give him the complete and unquestioning trust he gave his mother.

Tony knew that all his father needed was *one good break.* Tony wasn't exactly sure what *one good break* was. Whenever his father's union went out on strike, and whenever his father began to come home at odd hours with that grim, yet sometimes triumphant look a picket line brings, Tony thought this might be the beginning of *one good break.* But it never turned out that way, and Tony never got to know what it was. Yet he knew that the lack of it accounted partially for his father's lack of sympathy on certain occasions. He felt it would be a lot easier for his father if he didn't have to read Miss Clatt's letter.

But Tony also knew Miss Clatt. A good part of his existence was spent in anticipating Miss Clatt's moves and keeping one step ahead of them. He knew that Miss Clatt would have been most careful to ask for a reply in that letter. He also knew that if his father didn't read the letter, he and Miss Clatt were in for a long and unpleasant struggle. So he braced his shoulders, and when he got home he gave the letter to his mother.

"It's for Pop," he said.

"Tony, have you been in trouble again?"

He shook his head silently and his mother gave him a slice of bread and butter and sent him out to play. He went into the back yard, but it felt cold and was full of afternoon shadows, and the two little Santini sisters were playing house there. So he knew it was no use to think about the door today, and he went out to the street in front and found a game of one-o-cat instead.

After supper that night, Tony's father said, "Come on into your room, son. We'll have a talk."

"All right."

They went into his room, his father first, Tony following. Glancing back over his shoulder, Tony saw his mother watching them worriedly, drying her hands on a dish towel. Her black hair was drawn back, tight and shining. Even in just that moment, Tony thought of how lovely his mother's hair was. It was a shame that she couldn't hold him in as high esteem as he held her.

Tony sat on the bed and his father sat on the single chair in the room. Tony could see that his father was disturbed and did not know exactly how to begin to say what he wanted to say. Finally, he said, "You know how much I depend on you, Tony?"

"Uh-huh."

"Maybe if Mom and I had a lot of children, it would be different. But we only have you. I want you to get the breaks when you grow up. That's why I work so hard."

"I know, Pop."

"So how do you think I feel when I get a letter from your teacher that you've been lying again?"

"I guess you feel pretty bad, Pop."

"And such a stupid lie—to tell your teacher that you know a bunch of Indians. What made you do that?"

"Because it's true. And she told us a lot of things about Indians that aren't true and I knew that, so I told her."

"How did you know that what she said about the Indians wasn't true?"

"Because I know these Indians and they're good friends of mine," Tony answered.

"What Indians?"

"The Wesquaesteek."

"Tony, I don't want you inventing any stories for me. I'm sick and tired of your lies."

"But I tell you, Pop, I'm not lying and I wasn't lying to Miss Clatt. I walked up to their village with Peter Van Doben."

"Who is Peter Van Doben?"

Tony swallowed, took a deep breath, and said, "The Dutch boy."

"What Dutch boy?"

"They have a farm and he's a friend of mine."

"Tony, that's enough. Don't you understand what you're saying? Indian village, farm, Dutch boy—one lie after another. Why? Do you expect me to believe these stories?"

"No," said Tony. "I guess not."

"Then why do you tell them?"

"Because they're true," Tony said hopelessly.

That was the point where his father began to get angry. "What do you mean, they're true? I know they're not true. Is a licking the only thing that's going to help you, Tony? How can you sit there and tell me that you've been to an Indian village and a Dutch farm? Where are they?"

"Outside," said Tony miserably, motioning toward the window.

"Tony!"

"I go through the door in the yard," Tony said quickly, wanting to get it out and have it over with. "I go through the door in the yard and then I come out in the barnyard of Peter Van Doben's farm. Then everything is different. There are just farms and woods and no tenement houses or streets, and when you go up the road to the northern end of the island, that's where the Indian village is. It's right in a little hollow that runs across the island, down to the North River. You climb down into the hollow, and the Indians have made a road there, just a little cart road through the woods, and when you run down that road, the dogs begin to bark. The road is full of sunshine coming through the leaves, and the dogs are yellow, almost the same color as the sunshine, and they leap all around you but never bite, and only lick your hand. And then you see the village, with all the bark houses and the smell of good things cooking, and the big piles of white shells everywhere, and the Dutch traders, buying furs and smoking their little pipes all the time . . ."

"Tony, that's enough! I don't want to hear any more!"

"But you asked me. You asked me to tell you."

"Lies?"

Tony stared at his father.

"Do you see," said Tony's father, more gently now, "how one lie leads into another and how complicated you can make it, son? It's better not to start, isn't it?"

"I guess so."

"But what's in your mind when you tell those stories? We both know that the door in the fence leads into the next yard. Isn't that so, Tony?"

Tony shook his head. Worse than anything, he hated to get into something like this with his father. Now that he had told about the door, he had to make his father understand that he was telling the truth.

"It leads into Peter Van Doben's farm," he insisted.

His father stood up and pointed a large finger at him and said, "All right, Tony. That does it. You and I are going out into the yard right now. We're going through that door. And if it's what I say it is, I'm going to teach you that lies don't pay. Come along now."

Tony came. They marched silently through the kitchen, past his mother, down the stairs, out the back door, and into the yard. The yard was dark, lit faintly by splashes of light from windows. Tony and his father picked their way through the rubbish to the door in the fence.

"Open it," Tony's father said.

Tony opened it, and there was the yard of the next house, familiar piles of rubbish, and the looming red wall of another tenement. For a long moment, the two of them, Tony and his father, stood there looking at the cluttered yard. Then Tony's father closed the door in the fence and led Tony back to the house. They were going up the stairs when he said, "We'll forget about the licking, son. Just say you're sorry and that there'll be no more lies."

"It wasn't a lie. I knew it wouldn't work when you opened the door. It didn't work because you didn't believe me."

"You're going to insist that you weren't lying, Tony?"

"I wasn't lying."

"Then I guess the licking is the only way. I've got to make you understand this."

It was a long time before Tony was able to fall asleep that night, and while he lay in bed, dry-eyed and unhappy, his mother and father sat in the kitchen and talked.

"It's the first real licking you ever gave him," said Tony's mother.

"Yes, and I hated to do it, but how else was I going to convince him of what he was doing? He tells those lies so well now I sometimes think he believes them himself. For a moment, he almost had me believing him, and that's bad. He'll get so he can't tell the difference between what is a lie and what is the truth."

"But he's a good boy."

"Sure, he's a good boy, and I want him to stay that way. Can you imagine, telling that story about the Indians and even inventing a name for them! Wesquaesteek."

"What?" asked Tony's mother.

"That's the name he gave the Indians—Wesquaesteek. You've got to admit he has imagination."

"I agree with you. But I don't think you should be so upset about his imagination. It seems to me that the first thing a man does is to forget that he was ever a little boy himself. You always recognize that it's hard for you and for the man on the job with you. Why don't you recognize that it's hard for Tony—or for any child to grow up in a neighborhood like this one?"

A while later, Tony's father put on his jacket and said he was going downstairs for a breath of fresh air and a cigar. But his breath of fresh air took him to the office of old Doc Forbes, the neighborhood physician, whose hobby was Indian tribes and Indian relics.

Old Doc Forbes was one-quarter Indian, and whenever he took a vacation, he was off to learn something about that quarter of himself. He had visited Indian reservations all over America, and he had even written a book on the subject himself. Now Tony's father found him sitting in his little study, wearing slippers and a smoking jacket, and reading a book about the Iroquois Confederation. He sighed as he laid down his book and took off his glasses.

"Hello, Levy. Is it the wife or Tony?"

"Neither. We're all fine and healthy for a change. I want to ask you a question about Indians."

Old Doc Forbes smiled with relief and put on his glasses again. "Good. Sit down and make yourself comfortable. Have Indians been disturbing Mott Street?"

"Not for a long time, I guess," answered Tony's father, sitting down in a deep and comfortable chair. "But when they were, back in the old times, what Indians would they have been?"

Old Doc Forbes nodded and chuckled to himself. "If that's your problem, Levy, you put your finger on one of the knottiest ones in this whole field of Indian study. Actually, there's nothing as mixed up and puzzling as the Indian tribes in the days when the Dutch settled Manhattan Island. We know very little about it, and what we do know is just as likely as not wrong. Take the first question, one of the respected legends of old citizens like myself—that Peter Minuit bought Manhattan Island from the Indians for twenty-four dollars. Now in his own journal, he entered the purchase as being made from the *Carnarsie* Indians, and ever since then New Yorkers have had a good laugh over a Brooklyn tribe selling something they never owned—the first confidence game ever played on this island. But of course neither the Carnarsies nor any other Indians ever sold Manhattan Island."

"Why not?" asked Tony's father.

"Because they never owned it. No tribe in this area had the slightest knowledge of what ownership of land meant, and they couldn't have sold something they didn't have.

"So the Carnarsies were not swindlers at all, but took old Minuit's gift for what it was worth. They couldn't speak Dutch and he couldn't speak Indian, so they thought it was a gift and accepted it as that. Anyway, they were subject to the Six Nations—the *Iroquois*. So were the *Montauks* and the *Rockaways,* although the *Raritans* out on Staten Island might possibly not have been of *Algonquin* stock.

"You know, there's another legend to add to the reputation of this old town of ours, that the Raritans had swindling in their blood, since they sold Staten Island at least five times to five different parties. But, actually, like the other Indian tribes of the time, they hadn't the least idea that they were selling anything.

"This was *Mohawk* territory, in a way of speaking, and all of these little local tribes were periodically subject to pay tribute to the Mohawks."

"Hold on, please, Dr. Forbes," Tony's father said, realizing that if Tony knew even one quarter as much as this, he had better change some of his thinking about his son. "You said Six Nations and then Iroquois. What were the Six Nations and what were the Iroquois?"

"Both the same thing," Doc Forbes said and laughed. "It's a shame, but people don't know much about the first Americans, the Indians, these days. The Six Nations were a confederation of six important tribes—let's see if I can name them from memory. There were the *Cayugas,* the *Onondagas,* the *Mohawks,* of course, the *Senecas,* the *Oneidas,* and—now what is that last tribe?—yes, the *Tuscarroras.*"

"You mean the Indians had a United States of their own?"

"Only in a manner of speaking. Many people believe that it is only when tribes begin to league themselves into a confederation and actually form a nation that they can make the next step toward a real civilization, the building of cities and so forth. Well, the Iroquois were on their way when the white man came. They had a good working political confederacy. They built great wooden houses and public halls. They planted crops. And, naturally, all this made them powerful enough to impose their will on neighbor tribes—even all the way down here to Mott Street."

"And what do you mean by Algonquin stock?"

"That's a language grouping. We give it to those Indian tribes who seem to speak related languages, trying that way to trace broad movements and migrations."

"But what tribes were actually on Manhattan Island?" Tony's father insisted.

"That, too, is a matter of dispute," said old Doc Forbes. "Take the name *Manhattan*—you'll find books that tell you it means this and that, *Island of Mountains, Great Whirlpool*—many things. But those are guesses. All we really know about the name is that a small tribe of Indians who lived somewhere near where 42nd Street is today had a name something like that . . ."

"The *Manhattans*," Tony's father interrupted.

"Or *Mannahattans* or *Mannahootans* or something like that. We don't really know. But you look relieved."

"I am relieved," said Tony's father. "They were the only tribe here, you say?"

"Not at all," said old Doc Forbes. "There was a much larger and stronger tribe which had villages from the Bronx to Washington Heights . . ."

"Wait a minute," interrupted Tony's father. "Did they call themselves the *Wesquaesteek?*"

"*Wesquaesteek*," repeated old Doc Forbes with sudden interest. "That's a new pronunciation, but a more logical one than what we have. We usually spell the name *Weckquaesgeek*—which makes it almost unpronounceable. Where did you hear that pronunciation?"

"Someday I'll tell you," said Tony's father. "But I suppose

you could learn all about them in the Public Library."

"If you were a good scholar, you might locate the name," said old Doc Forbes. "There really isn't any more than that which we know—except that they were unusually gentle and just folk, good people, you might say."

"I see," said Tony's father, and then he rose, said good-by, and walked home.

"Did you get the cigar?" asked Tony's mother, as he entered the house.

"As a matter of fact, I forgot all about it."

Then he went into Tony's room. Tony was asleep. The moonlight poured in through the window, and as Tony slept, he smiled, as if he were seeing very unusual things indeed.

❧ 2 ❧

Tony and old Doc Forbes

Miss Clatt was a patient and much harassed woman. In her crowded class, she had forty-four live and active children, so she was not to be blamed any more than Tony was to be blamed. With forty-three children she probably could have coped successfully; the forty-fourth was the straw that broke the camel's back, and the forty-fourth was also Tony MacTavish Levy.

So on this sunny day, a few days after her last encounter with Tony, she could be pardoned for being annoyed at Tony's dreamy concentration through the window. Dreaminess had spread among the children like a disease, for this was the first pleasant, sunny day of spring, a boon to youth but quite the reverse to those who instruct youth.

Therefore, Miss Clatt lectured, but Tony's thoughts were apart from her subject.

Miss Clatt: "Captain Hendrick Hudson sailed his ship, the

Half Moon past Sandy Hook and into the Lower Bay during September 1609."

Tony: I wonder what kind of a tree that scrawny old tree I see through the window is?

Miss Clatt: "The *Half Moon* ventured as far as Castle Island."

Tony: I guess it's a plane tree. I guess that's the only kind of a tree that would grow on Mott Street.

Miss Clatt: "You see, Captain Hudson was seeking that mythical sea passage through our continent."

Tony: There's a sparrow. Now that's a funny little bird. Doesn't seem to matter how cold it is, you always find sparrows in New York City.

Miss Clatt: "His *Half Moon* was the first European ship ever to sail into the North River."

Tony: I know what it's called—it's called an English sparrow, and I guess it did come over from England. I can't remember ever seeing such a bird on the other side of the door. Now what kind of birds do I see there?

Miss Clatt: "But, you see, when Captain Hudson realized that the inlet was only a river, not a sea passage, his greatest dream was shattered."

Tony: Let me see—there are a lot of birds on the other side of the door. I can remember lots of them—thrashers and bluebirds and robins and thrushes and catbirds and creepers and nuthatches and vireos and hummingbirds and woodpeckers.

Miss Clatt went on talking and Tony went on dreaming until the teacher suddenly said, "Tony!"

Tony: But no English sparrows, which goes to prove that they were brought over from England. Now just suppose that one of those sparrows flew through the door with me, and then it would be there when it wasn't there, and then it wouldn't have to be brought over from England at all.

Miss Clatt, much louder and sharper: "Tony!"

Dreaminess was not limited to Tony. Each and every one of forty-three other assorted children had caught his or her share of spring fever; but they demonstrated this by twisting and turning and scratching and craning and whispering and grimacing. If Tony had only done one or several of these things, Miss Clatt would have endured it patiently. It was Tony's fixed, trancelike stare through the window which had prompted Miss Clatt's impatient summons.

"Yes? Yes, Miss Clatt?" Tony awoke.

Miss Clatt had carried her lecture many generations past the discovery of the North River by Captain Hudson. She had just asked a question, and now she said severely, "Tony, if you heard my question, please answer it."

Miss Clatt's question concerned Wall Street and the building of the wall from which it derived its name. Miss Clatt had just finished telling the class how, long, long ago, when New York was just a Dutch village, Peter Stuyvesant had built the wall along its length, from river to river, so that the Dutch settlers might be able to defend themselves against the Indians. After that, her question referred to the wall and why it was built.

All Tony caught was some mention of the wall, and he came to life, answering forthrightly, "They didn't need the wall against the Indians. The Indians never bothered anyone until Mynheer Van Dyck murdered poor Dramaque—for one peach. He was a bad man. If they had turned him over to the Indians the way Peter's father said, there wouldn't have been any trouble and they wouldn't have needed any wall."

"What on earth are you talking about?" exclaimed Miss Clatt.

"The wall on Wall Street."

"And what, Tony Levy, has all that nonsense got to do with the wall on Wall Street?"

"I thought you asked me why they built the wall in the first place," said Tony, "And I was explaining that the old man— that is, Peg Leg Stuyvesant—built it because he was so suspicious and afraid of the Indians. But the Dutch settlers didn't need a wall. Mynheer Van Dyck had no right to shoot a woman for a peach. Everyone is always ready to blame everything on the Indians, but suppose . . ."

The class was roaring with laughter now, and Miss Clatt, in desperation, cried, "That will be quite enough, Tony!"

Tony was out playing when Miss Clatt came to see his mother that afternoon. Miss Clatt thought it was necessary to make a special call. As she explained to Mrs. Levy, "If he were just the usual type of bad boy, I wouldn't bother. I would know how to handle him, I think."

"Tony isn't a bad boy," said Mrs. Levy.

"He isn't. Of course he isn't a bad boy, but he has a very vivid imagination, and he tells the most outrageous lies. I don't know where they come from or where he gets his information, but the result is that he undermines the discipline of the class."

And he makes me look like a fool, Miss Clatt thought to herself, but she couldn't say that.

"We've had trouble with that," Mrs. Levy nodded. "I don't know why he does it, because in every other way he's a good boy."

And maybe in this way, too, Tony's mother thought to herself. She resented Miss Clatt's saying that Tony was a liar. People who didn't understand children were quick to call them liars, but very often the world of their imagination was real to them, and they were not really lying when they described it. She wondered whether her husband was right in saying that people like Miss Clatt would never really have enough time and love for children so long as they allowed themselves to be pushed around. She knew how low and miserable a teacher's wages were, and she wondered whether so simple an answer could be right.

"Now in our history lesson today," Miss Clatt began, and then went on to tell exactly what had happened. "And he speaks with such assurance," she finished.

Tony's mother thought of the door in the wall, which Tony's father had told her about. She was almost tempted to tell Miss Clatt about that, but at the last moment she decided not to. Afterwards, she realized that the reason she kept silent about Tony's wonderful door was because of a deep suspicion that Miss Clatt might laugh. And Tony's mother felt very strongly that no one had any right to laugh at that.

"It has to stop," Miss Clatt said firmly.

"It will stop," Tony's mother agreed. "I'll talk to his father about it."

"That's not enough," said Miss Clatt. "I think you ought to get help."

"Help? What kind of help? We've never needed help with Tony."

"Medical help," said Miss Clatt, nodding her head.

"Are you intimating that there's something wrong with Tony? There's nothing wrong with him. He's a healthy boy. He has too much imagination, that's all."

"Still . . . it's best to nip these things in the bud," said Miss Clatt. "I would think about it."

"I shall," said Tony's mother coldly.

And after Miss Clatt left, she thought about it a good deal.

While this was going on, Tony sat on the bedspring in the back yard, studying the door. It was a very ordinary door, built of pine boards which were held together by stringers on top and bottom and a plank nailed from corner to corner on a slant. Tony was somewhat puzzled by the fact that the other side of the door, when he saw it from Peter Van Doben's father's barn-yard, had precisely the same construction. He thought this strange when he considered that every other door around the Van Doben place was of Dutch design; built in two parts, one above the other, two separate doors in one doorway.

This one, however, was an ordinary board door in a fence; and looking at it, Tony had to admit that it was by no means an unusual door. It led from this yard into the facing yard of the house on the next street, and it had been built at a time when such a passage must have been both desirable and convenient. Long since, any such door had become unnecessary; the iron latch had become stiff and rusty and the metal hinges creaked loudly and complainingly whenever the door was opened. Like the fence around it, the door was painted green, a faded, streaked green. This peculiar color is found nowhere in the whole world except on the fences of New York City back yards, just as the little ailanthus, growing so cheerfully through the old bedspring, was also known as the tree of the New York back yards.

Of course, Tony admitted to himself, any reasonable person, especially those astonishingly unreasonably reasonable folk who are no longer children, but grown, would be convinced that if you opened that door, you would see nothing except the yard on the other side of the fence. That is exactly what had happened when his father opened the door. On the other hand, however, it was just as natural to Tony's way of thinking for the door to lead not only into an entirely different scene, but an entirely different time as well.

The question of place and time had never really puzzled Tony. You could open that door a thousand times and every time you might see only the ordinary pile of rubbish which was native to all back yards in that neighborhood. He had done so himself any number of times. But then there came the day when he had a certain kind of a feeling, and since then he had never opened the door unless he had exactly that kind of feeling. The first time he had that feeling, he had walked straight over to the door and opened it—and there it was. He was not surprised; he was not puzzled; he was not even disturbed. It was completely natural that the door should suddenly be a magic door instead of an ordinary door. It was just as natural that the door should lead far back into the past, into a past when of all the places on earth, Manhattan Island was one of the loveliest. That Manhattan was not covered all over with tall and ugly buildings and threaded with dirty streets, but quilted instead with green pastures, dense forests, and little Dutch farms.

Tony never told anyone how much he wanted green fields and woods, how much he disliked the jungle of pushcarts on Hester Street and Allen Street, the crowds of people, the dirt, the din of shouts. He dreamed of a place like that behind the door. And then he found the door.

Of all the things in his whole life, Tony admitted, the most wonderful was the wonderful magic door. Why, he asked himself, had he ever told anyone of the door? He had an instinctive feeling that the way through the door was precarious. A delicate balance was involved, and even talking about it might upset it—and talking about it to people who neither believed nor understood was even worse.

Yet the reasonableness of the door was such that he couldn't resist talking about it. Take this moment, for instance. There it was, right in front of him. Here he was and, inside of him, right inside of him, Tony MacTavish Levy was beginning to get that funny feeling of excitement and expectancy and delicious anticipation. It was when he felt this way that he knew what the door held. He had no doubts at all about what would follow if he opened the door now.

He sprawled lazily on the bedspring. From the street, he

heard the voices of children racing past in play, but instead of wanting to be with them, he felt rather sorry for them. How could any games of theirs compare to his magic door? Nor was any one of them as good and trusting a friend as Peter Van Doben.

What, he wondered, would Peter be doing right this moment? Well, there was no way of answering that question without looking for himself. Tony got up and went to the door. Smiling in anticipation, he opened it and passed through.

"Miss Clatt is an old busybody," said Tony's father when he came home that evening and heard his wife's story.

"Whatever she is," said Mrs. Levy, "she has her own problems, and Tony is one of them now."

"Why does he lie like that?" asked Tony's father.

"Maybe it isn't lying to him," said Tony's mother. "You know the way kids are."

"I know—but other kids aren't that way. Other kids play . . ."

"So does Tony."

"With that door, and with those lies. What kind of man will he grow up into, telling such terrible lies?"

"They're not such terrible lies."

"They are," said Tony's father, "and they make me ashamed. I could understand his lying if he had to lie. It wouldn't be right, but at least I could understand a lie if he lied to escape punishment. But he seems to lie just for the pleasure of it—and what is worse than anything is that he becomes so convincing that I almost begin to believe him myself. Every time I look at that door now, I get a funny feeling."

"I know," nodded Tony's mother. "But that doesn't mean he's crazy, and it's no use being foolish about the door. It's just a game, and he'll forget it soon enough."

"And you don't think he ought to see a doctor?"

"Of course not. He's a healthy boy, isn't he? He's a good boy, too. Where is he now, I wonder?"

As if in answer to Mr. Levy's question, Tony entered. His pants were torn at the knee; one stocking was up, the other down. He was flushed, excited, and full of irrepressible triumph, and across his cheek was a long red scratch.

"Hello, Pop," he said. "Hello, Mom."

"Fighting, Tony?" his father asked.

"Nope."

"Where'd you get that scratch?"

"Just got it," Tony said and shrugged.

"Any reason why you shouldn't tell me how?"

"You wouldn't believe me," Tony answered.

"Why shouldn't I believe you?"

"Because I got it on the other side of the door."

"What door?" asked Tony's father quietly.

"The door in the yard."

"You mean you got it in the yard next door?"

Tony hesitated; then he said, "No—I got it playing *sum-wo* with the Indians."

"That," said Tony's father, "decides it. We'll go to see old Doc Forbes tonight."

Tony liked old Doc Forbes, just as most of the children on Mott Street liked him. Some men, as they grow old, grow away from children; others, like old Doc Forbes, grow toward them.

Now Tony and his father sat in old Doc Forbes' study, with all his diplomas and Indian relics around on the walls, and all his books and all his jars and bottles with their strange specimens making a fine background for him. Doc Forbes sat in his big black leather chair, with the stuffing coming out here and there, not from him but from the chair, and with dust on the chair as well as everywhere else; for he was a widower and his house reflected it.

His glasses were pushed up on his forehead, and his pudgy hands were folded over his round and respectable stomach, and he regarded Tony with interest and not a little admiration.

"Suppose Tony and I have a talk, by ourselves," old Doc Forbes said to Mr. Levy. "Suppose you sit down outside in my waiting room and read the *National Geographic* while Tony

and I have a good man-to-man talk about this door. Nothing I like better than talking about doors—especially the kind that open. All too many are kept locked these days."

Tony's father was somewhat relieved at the suggestion, and he went out into the waiting room and began to read all about Tibet in the *National Geographic,* while old Doc Forbes grinned at Tony and got out a box of gumdrops.

"I keep them hidden," he explained. "Just out of habit. I used to hide them from my two daughters who were always complaining about my waistline. Now they're married and my waistline's gone, but I keep them hidden out of habit. Have some purple ones; they're anise. So nobody believes you about the door?"

"I guess not," Tony said, his mouth full of gumdrops.

"As I understand it," said old Doc Forbes, very seriously and with no trace of mockery in his voice, "it happens this way. You get to feel a certain way, and then you have no doubts at all about that door. You open it up and go through it, and then you come out in the barnyard of Peter Van Doben, and that's a long, long time ago. Way back when New York was just a little Dutch village. Is that the way it is, Tony?"

"Yes, sir," nodded Tony.

"That would place the Van Doben farm just about where Mott Street cuts into Houston Street these days. It might be checked at that," said old Doc Forbes. Though after that earlier explanation about the Indian tribe, he was not certain of the value of checking on Tony's facts. "It was a farm, Tony?"

"You would call it a farm, Dr. Forbes. Peter doesn't."

"What does he call it, Tony?"

"A *bouwerie*," answered Tony, and Dr. Forbes swallowed several times and then held out the gumdrops to Tony. Tony selected two purple ones and a green one, and chewed them with evident relish. He felt more comfortable than he had in a long time.

"Now this trouble in Miss Clatt's class today," said old Doc Forbes, "it started with Wall Street. As I understand it, you told her there shouldn't have been any necessity for the wall if only that fool and blackguard Van Dyck hadn't murdered that poor Indian woman. I agree with you, although certain people who pretend to know a great deal about early New York claim that the wall was built before this particular incident. All this you could have gotten by spending an hour in the Public Library; but I understand you knew what her name was, which is something none of us have ever known."

"Everyone knew her name," said Tony. "Peter told me about it the day after it happened. Her name was *Dramaque* . . . "

"An Algonquin name," thought old Doc Forbes. He had always suspected that there were Algonquin Indians on Manhattan Island; but a moment later he was laughing at himself for falling into Tony's game.

". . . and she was a *sachem's* daughter," went on Tony.

"Wait a minute!" cried old Doc Forbes, losing his objective attitude for the first time. "They didn't have sachems, not among the Wesquaesteek."

"But they did," insisted Tony. "I know because that was when the sachems came from the Iroquois, because the old man sent for them."

"What old man?"

"Stuyvesant—that's what Peter, my Dutch friend, always calls him, the old man."

"You go on eating those gumdrops," said old Doc Forbes, going to the sideboard and pouring a brandy for himself. He swallowed quickly, put the brandy bottle away, and then turned to Tony, directing a pudgy finger at him.

"I will admit that rumor has it that three sachems of the Iroquois visited Peter Stuyvesant at his request. But I never put any stock in it. Why should they?"

"I don't know," said Tony. "I only know that I saw them."

"Where? Through that confounded door of yours, I suppose?"

Tony nodded. "Their war canoe was on the canal," he said hopelessly, thinking that now old Doc Forbes would be just like all the rest of them.

Meanwhile, old Doc Forbes was delivering a lecture to himself. There you go, he said to himself. Losing your temper

over this little boy's fantasy. How can you help him if you begin
to shout at him? The thing to do is to puncture his story. Prick
it. Let it deflate itself. Show him that all of this simply exists in
his active mind and nowhere else. Don't call him a liar, but do
it the sensible way.

Having said all that to himself, old Doc Forbes seated himself in his black leather chair again and helped himself to
another gumdrop. "Well, Tony," he said, "that's a wonderful
door you have, a wonderful door indeed. I'd like to step through
it myself. Of course, one would have certain language difficul-
ties. They would speak Dutch, wouldn't they? I mean even
your friend, Peter Van Doben, would speak Dutch, wouldn't
he?"

"That's right," said Tony.

"So you couldn't speak to him unless you knew Dutch!"

"Uh-huh," Tony nodded.

"But you don't speak Dutch, do you?" asked old Doc Forbes.

"A little," said Tony. "I learned some Dutch and he learned
some English and we talk to each other that way."

"I see," said old Doc Forbes, never batting an eyelash.
"Then you could talk to me in Dutch?"

"Do you know Dutch?" asked Tony.

"I speak German and understand Dutch, so if you were to
say something, I would know it. Suppose you ask me what my
name is."

"*Hoe beet U?*" said Tony.

Old Doc Forbes half-choked, swallowed rapidly two or three times and once again reached for the gumdrops.

"*Hoe meakt U bet?*" said Tony.

"What?"

"I'm sorry," said Tony. "You didn't look so good, and I asked you how you were and I spoke Dutch without thinking."

"That's a very wonderful door," said old Doc Forbes slowly. "Wonderful enough to make me forget about being a doctor for a while. That's a nasty scratch on your face, Tony. Let me swab it out."

Feeling a desperate necessity to change the subject, old Doc Forbes got out of his chair, found a bottle of peroxide, and washed out the scratch on Tony's face.

"How did it happen?" he asked Tony.

"Playing sum-wo."

"Sum-wo?"

"It's a game the Indians play," Tony explained uneasily. "Today, Peter and I went up to their village. First they wouldn't let us play. Then they did. That's how I got the scratch."

"How do you play sum-wo?" old Doc Forbes asked.

"You play it with a ball," said Tony. "The ball is about the size of a big orange, and there are twenty-two players on each team, and sometimes the children play it and sometimes the big people play it, but always the *patria* throws up the ball for the game to begin."

"What did you call him?"

"The patria—that's what Peter and his father call him. He's an old, old man, and he's the father of the whole village. He has almost nothing to do but sit in the sunshine outside his lodge and decide arguments—especially when the kids have arguments—and sometimes he will start a game, like sum-wo. *Pata-lo,* they call him, but Peter and me, we call him patria, and he gives us little bits of fish that taste like candy because they're cooked in maple syrup. Well, he starts the game by throwing the ball into the air, and some one catches the ball in his stick and throws it."

"What is the stick like, Tony?" old Doc Forbes interrupted.

"Well, it's just a hickory stick that's bent at one end like a cane, and then there's a rawhide net from the bent part back to the stick, and you use that to catch the ball and throw it."

"Lacrosse, of course. Where have you seen lacrosse played, Tony?"

"I don't know what lacrosse is," Tony said, "but they let Peter and me play today, and that's how I got this scratch."

For a long time, old Doc Forbes sat there, his head cocked, scratching his bald spot and regarding Tony quizzically. Finally, he said, "Let's finish the gumdrops, Tony."

They both munched gumdrops, and when the last one was

gone, old Doc Forbes slid his glasses down on his nose, studied Tony a moment more, and then said, "Going back through the door?"

"You won't tell?"

"You'd be surprised at how many secrets I've got locked away in this old head of mine."

"I guess I am," Tony confessed.

"What would happen if you brought something back with you?"

"Through the door?" asked Tony.

"Uh-huh."

"It doesn't seem right," said Tony.

"You know I collect Indian things," said old Doc Forbes. "Now a pair of those sticks would be a fine thing for me to have, and maybe a ball to go with them."

Tony looked at him blankly.

"Just think it over, Tony. Just think it over, and if you should feel like doing an old codger like me a favor, why I'd appreciate it mightily. Now suppose you run along home, while I have a few words with your father."

But just as Tony was going out, old Doc Forbes stopped him, with a question that made old Doc Forbes feel a lot more foolish than a substantial family physician like himself had any right to feel.

"Tony," he said, "you remember telling me that three Iroquois sachems came down the river to visit old Peg Leg Stuyvesant?"

"He couldn't stand being called Peg Leg. Some of the children called him that and he took after them with his cane."

"Yes—but about those sachems. How were they dressed? You say you saw them?"

"They wore long cloaks," Tony answered, wrinkling his brow and trying to remember very exactly. "White deerskin, I guess. They didn't look the way we think of Indians looking. Their cloaks made you think of kings, the way they were embroidered all over with beads and bits of horn. They wore leggings. Their hair was long and white as snow."

"And feathers on their heads, I suppose?"

"No—oh, no," said Tony. "No feathers. They wore things that were like crowns, only I guess they were made of wood, and on each side, a deer's horn was mounted. You know the pictures of Norsemen you see—well, that is what they reminded me of . . ."

"Children," said old Doc Forbes to Tony's father, "live in a world of their own. It touches our world at certain given points, but the relationship is one of necessity, not of desire. The trouble with us is that we not only forget that world in the rush of trying to earn a living and keep a roof over our heads, but we

47

reject it as well, and often enough reject the children with it."

"Then you don't think Tony is crazy?"

"Nonsense! He's as sane as you or I, and maybe even saner. He needs understanding and affection. Don't you see what he's done? There are certain things which he doesn't get in this world of Mott Street, so he has created a world of his own. You or I go through that door, and we come into a yard full of rubbish. He goes through it and he comes out where for some reason he would like to be, in New York of almost three hundred years ago. And with his vivid, active imagination, he has populated it with creations who stay as close to reality as he can have them. In a way, it's a very wonderful thing he has done, and there's a world of minute detail of old New Amsterdam which he has put together. But there's nothing that can't be explained and no information which might not be gathered in some public library or in the movies. And I don't think I'd be guessing wrong if I guessed that Tony has been spending all too many hours in dusty old books right there at the library."

"And what do I do about it?" asked Tony's father. "I can't have him telling those lies to anyone who'll listen to him."

"In the first place, to him they are not lies. He sees these things in his own mind—in a way that only children can—and to him they represent the truth. Just as much of the truth as a lot of things we believe in. The difference is that we'll go to our grave believing in the same smoky illusions, while one day

Tony will open his door and see nothing but a dirty yard through it. And then he'll be none the worse, so my advice is to do absolutely nothing about it."

But when Tony's father had gone home, saying the same "Thank you, Doctor," which old Doc Forbes had heard for almost half a century now, the doctor reseated himself in his black leather armchair, pushed his glasses up onto his brow, closed his eyes, and thought of Tony MacTavish Levy's wonderful door.

It was amazing what illusions that little boy could create, with his matter-of-fact and unhesitating answers to any question. It took old Doc Forbes back to his own childhood, so long, long ago. He had been born in New York at a time when the upper half of Manhattan Island was still a place of meadows, woods, and pleasant little farms. In those days, if you took a carriage and drove to Fort George Hill or to Inwood, you were driving out into the country. It was very pleasant country indeed, just as nice, with all its little hills and valleys and brooks, as any in the whole world. If you stood on the rocky bluff of Fort Tryon in those times, you could look all around you and see nothing but the blue and green hills, except far away in the south where the city was.

But that, old Doc Forbes reflected, was all gone today, all covered over with city streets and tenements. Unlike Tony, he had no doors which he could open and which he could use to revisit those scenes of his own childhood.

In the eighteen-nineties, a tiny tribe of Indians still lived in the lush valley which opened onto Spuyten Duyvil. As a boy, old Doc Forbes had visited them often enough, and there had begun his lifelong interest in things Indian, in the habits and lives of those red men who had lived in this land, once long, long ago, and ruled it, too. Actually, he did not regret the past. He was much too alive and interested in the present; and he loved his city in a way that few people did. But he couldn't help thinking what a splendid thing it would be to have the use of Tony's door, if only for one single time.

"Well," he said aloud and to no one in particular, "I'll be darned if I'm not beginning to believe that lad."

Doc Forbes was fully aware that he was much too old and much too practical and possessed much too large a practice of much too poor people to believe one word about Tony Mac-Tavish Levy's magic door for even one moment. Therefore, he laid all such nonsense aside and turned to a large, dull, green, totally uninspiring book on internal medicine—a book that was well calculated to put anyone's imagination to rest.

Yet his thoughts kept leaping back to the door, and finally he closed his book, picked up the telephone, and called the house of an old crony of his. This old friend, whose name was Isaac Gilman, was curator at the Museum of the American

Indian. He spent most of his time working at the museum, worrying about exhibits. He kept moving them from place to place for no reason at all, carrying some down to the basement, carrying others up to the cases, and brooding over the fact that his museum didn't have enough money to buy new exhibits. If he only had new exhibits he could carry more old exhibits down to the basement.

Old Doc Forbes and Isaac Gilman were good friends. They could argue constantly and shout the most unbelievable and terrible things at each other, and still remain friends. And most of the time they argued about Indians.

Now, old Doc Forbes said to his friend over the telephone, "Ike, what would you say if I told you that the Wesquaesteek Indians played lacrosse?"

"I'd say you know less about Indians than even I thought you did."

"It couldn't be?"

"Absolutely not. No observer even indicated as much, and they could hardly have failed to notice any public display of that sort."

"Of course," said old Doc Forbes cannily, "you weren't there."

"Were you, you old idiot?" Ike Gilman shouted back. "Calling up a man in the middle of the night to find out if the Wesquaesteek played lacrosse!"

"Now just take it easy and watch your blood pressure," old Doc Forbes cautioned him. "Try to act like a scholar if not like a gentleman, and answer a question. What was the head-dress of a great lord of the Iroquois Confederation?"

"Any fool knows that."

"Not any fool—just you and me and a half dozen others. Now suppose you answer the question, as if you were talking real polite to a millionaire who might donate a new wing to that mausoleum of yours."

"All right, the crown is wood glued onto snakeskin and mounted with colored stones. Two deer horns, each with four prongs, are fixed like the wings of a Viking's helm. That led to a certain confusion, but it had nothing to do with the Vikings. Grew up out of the customs of the Iroquois Confederation."

"A very good, colorful description," said old Doc Forbes. "How many have you got in your collection?"

"None!" snapped Ike Gilman. "Nor has anyone else, as you well know, you old fool! I suppose you turned one up at a second-hand furniture store on Mott Street?"

"Nope—but I might turn up a couple of lacrosse sticks."

"Is that all you've got to annoy me with?"

"Seriously, though, how would one find out about the helm of an Iroquois lord?"

"Well, it's mentioned in a couple of monograph manuscripts and described in an article by the Historical Society. We also have an old engraving of it in our print collection. Morgan doesn't mention it, nor do any of the other authorities."

"You didn't happen to notice a small, freckle-faced boy ruffling through your prints?"

"What?"

"Never mind. One more question and you can go back and hibernate. Would a sachem wear that helm?"

"Absolutely not!"

"How do you know?"

"How do I know? That was the royal headdress of a great lord, not of a sachem. That's how I know."

Old Doc Forbes hung up the receiver and paced back and forth in his cluttered study. Finally, he said aloud but to no one at all, "*I'm* going to need a room in an insane asylum, not Tony MacTavish Levy."

At that moment, Tony MacTavish Levy was awakening from a dream in which he had chased a fat, squealing pig the whole length of Front Street. Chasing the pig with him were a number of other children, and they would have caught the pig, too, if the watchmaster hadn't seen them; then the chase reversed itself and Tony woke up.

In his dream, the watchmaster singled him out and was dashing after him with long, firm strides. Tony did not con-

sider that chasing a pig was so terrible a crime; but evidently
the watchmaster did. Tony ran full into Peter, and stood there
laughing and panting.

"Whew!" gasped Tony. "He almost caught me."

"Who?" Peter asked.

"Old Dooper De Groot, the cop," Tony said.

"But what is a cop?"

"They don't have watchmasters at home," Tony explained.

At that moment, he heard the wild roar of old Dooper De
Groot, who came into view with his big red mustache and his
wide-brimmed hat and his great, floppy boots and his enormous
curved sword and his red and yellow sash.

Tony woke up, and he lay there in his little brass bed in the darkness which was diffused somewhat by a glimmer of light from the kitchen through the open door, and he listened to his father and mother talking. He listened idly at first, the way a boy does whose eyes are all heavy with sleep—and then he listened more intently.

"It's all very well for old Doc Forbes to talk the way he does," Tony's father said. "Tony isn't his boy."

"But he likes Tony. You can't say that Tony doesn't mean anything to him."

"I'm not saying that. I'm not saying that Tony doesn't mean anything to Doc Forbes. I guess he thinks as much of Tony as he does of any other kids he takes care of. I'm just saying that Tony isn't his son."

"He's our son," Tony's mother said.

"Yes—that's just it. You can't blame me for wanting Tony to be everything I ever thought my son should be. Maybe if we had lots of money, it would be different. But we don't. Tony will have to make his own way."

"And why shouldn't he? Isn't he good and kind and intelligent?"

"Can't you see why? Those lies! He seems to tell those wild stories of his just for the love of telling them. What kind of a man will he grow up to be if he lies about everything?"

"You're not being fair," Tony's mother cried. "Tony's a

good boy. He doesn't lie about everything—only . . ."

"Only that door."

"All right. So he does make up stories about that old door. I don't see that it does such great harm."

"Maybe not," Tony's father muttered. He didn't want to admit that the door worried him, frightened him a little. Tony had made the door much too real to be comfortable. "Maybe not, but what's going to happen to the boy if he can't distinguish between what is truth and what isn't?"

"Perhaps you should have a talk with him again about the door."

"No. No, I've talked to him enough. I'll tell you what I've been thinking about doing. I've been thinking about getting some boards and nailing up that door so it can never be opened again."

It was at this point that Tony got out of bed and came into the kitchen, a small boy in pajamas, with a rumpled head of brown hair.

"You'd better not," he said. "You'd better not nail up my door. If you do, I'll go through it and I won't come back—ever."

 3

Tony and the Curator

On this day, Tony did not go to school. He did what was not uncommon on Mott Street, but what was fairly uncommon as a part of his own practice; he played hookey. And the peculiar part of it was that he did not clearly know why he did so.

The magic door had something to do with it. Tony almost meant what he said the night before—about going through the door and never coming back. That is, in one way he meant it, and in another way, he did not mean it at all. He loved his father and mother, and they were a very good pair of parents; but now he felt hurt and rejected by them. It made a lump of pain gather in his heart to think of leaving them and never coming back. Somehow or other, on the other side of the magic door, everyone understood him and everything happened just as he wanted it to happen.

Tony never remembered it raining on that old and lovely Manhattan he reached by going through the door. There the sun always shone, and old New Amsterdam nestled like a toy village on the lower tip of the Island, and Dutch boys and girls played all day long, and windmills turned, and fleecy white clouds blew across the sky. Everything there was just as it should be, just as Tony wanted it to be. And he thought of this today when he decided to stay home from school and go through the door.

But, in another way, it was something other than the door which was responsible. It did not seem to Tony that he could possibly face Miss Clatt and the children in his class again. And why should he face them, he asked himself? Therefore, Tony made his decision. And a part of his decision was to break open his small clay bank and fill his pockets with a lifetime's savings of pennies and nickles.

Tony's mother was worried. How could she explain to him that her gruffness and his father's gruffness and shortness were an expression of love and concern?

Nor could Tony share their alarm about his magic door. To him, the door was the very best and most exciting thing that had ever happened to him—and why should they worry about that?

In a way, his mother realized this. She wanted to tell Tony how much he meant to them, how completely he had become the object of all their hopes and ambitions. How do you explain such things to a little boy? she wondered.

On this morning Tony's mother had to visit her sister. Her sister was ill and she had two small children of her own.

How nice it would be to be able to do something for her sister. She thought about sending her and the children away to a place in the mountains, where they could just rest and sit in the sunshine. If only they weren't so poor.

Tony's father had just left for work. While Tony was dressing, his mother put out his morning bowl of oatmeal, his glass of milk, and his slice of bread and butter, and rehearsed in her mind what she would say to him. When Tony came in and sat down and began to eat, she sat opposite him, looking at him, at his round face and little snub nose, and loving him a great deal indeed.

She felt like crying, but instead she said, "You mustn't be angry at your father, Tony. He's very worried, and that's why he talks the way he does."

"He shouldn't have said he would nail up my door," Tony muttered.

"He didn't mean it. It's just that with so many other things to disturb him, he becomes more than a little upset when you talk about the door."

"I don't hurt anyone with the door," said Tony, his mouth full of hot oatmeal and sugar.

"But don't you see that your story is impossible, Tony? How

can you expect anyone to believe it?"

"Old Doc Forbes believes it. He even told me to bring something back through the door."

"Tony, please let's not talk about the door. I have to go to my sister's house and take care of the children. When you finish eating, put the dishes in the sink and hurry off to school."

Then she went away and left Tony alone, and he slowly and thoughtfully finished his breakfast. He put the dishes in the sink, picked up his books, and went down the stairs. But already he had decided that he would not go to school, and he went to the back yard instead.

He sat down on the bedspring in the sweet morning sunshine which flooded the yard. Sitting there, Tony did a good deal of thinking, and all the time he was thinking he kept looking at the door in the fence. Why did everyone react to the door with such bitter hostility—that is, everyone except old Doc Forbes? When you came right down to it, they seemed to act as if they were afraid of the door. And if they were afraid of the door, *why* were they afraid?

Tony himself was afraid of a good many things. Now, sitting in the sunshine of the back yard, he thought aloud of some of the things he was particularly afraid of.

"Twelve year old Mike Grady from up on Houston Street? Yes," he said. "I am afraid of him."

"Miss Clatt? Now I'm not really sure of that," he said. He

was not really afraid of Miss Clatt.

"Mom and Pop?" He was relieved to know that he was not afraid of them at all.

"The dark? Yes, and I am not ashamed to admit it," he said.

"Growing up?" he asked himself, and that made him pause and wonder a good deal. Was he afraid of growing up? "Do I want to grow up?" he wondered aloud. He shook his head perplexedly.

"Why shouldn't I want to grow up?" he asked aloud.

But there it was, the bitter truth of it—just edging into his mind with the knowledge that he didn't want to grow up.

He shrugged it off and looked at the door, the magic door, the old, weathered door of green boards, which was now shimmering all over with sunshine and glowing underneath with the promise of enchantment.

Tony stopped thinking about things which made his head ache. He leaped up, bounced several times on the old bedspring, directed his last bounce onto the old stove, circled the pile of tin cans, kicking one in passing, as he always did, bumped the broken dresser, and swung around the icebox. He darted along the rusty drainpipe, and took the wagon seat in one lusty leap. Three times he bounced on the old sofa before he hurdled it, threw open the magic door, and burst through.

The office hours of old Doc Forbes were from twelve until two o'clock, and in that time he usually saw upwards of twenty patients. Sometimes it discouraged him that the older he got, the bigger his practice became and the harder he had to work. He didn't earn more money, but he certainly did have more patients.

"And the worst part of it," he often said to himself, "is that I don't get any smarter."

As a matter of fact, it frequently seemed to old Doc Forbes that quite the reverse was true; for more and more he dreamed of the magic door of Tony MacTavish Levy, and more and more he found himself caught up in the dream world—as he saw it—of a small boy.

This was very much on his mind today as two o'clock arrived and his nurse informed him that only a small, snub-nosed boy was left.

"Is he sick?" asked old Doc Forbes.

"He seems less sick than out of breath. He acts the way he might if he had run a mile, and you can't be very sick if you are able to run a mile, can you?"

"Let's not argue about that. Just send him in," said old Doc Forbes. And he was not a bit surprised when Tony MacTavish Levy entered, both hands behind his back, and still panting a little from loss of breath. Old Doc Forbes felt that nothing Tony did or said from here on had any power to surprise him; but in that he was very much mistaken.

"Sick?" inquired old Doc Forbes.

"Nope."

"Holiday today?"

"Played hookey," Tony said firmly.

"What have you got behind your back?" asked old Doc Forbes. "A pair of lacrosse sticks?"

"I couldn't get them," said Tony, "so I brought this instead." And he held out in front of old Doc Forbes a deerhorn head-dress of a Great Lord of the Iroquois Confederation.

The staid exterior of the proper and elderly family physician vanished. His glasses slid down his nose, and he only caught them just in time and thrust them well up on his forehead, out of harm's way. Like a miser suddenly confronted with a topless tower of shining gold pieces, he held out two pudgy and trembling hands for the helm, took it from Tony, and almost drooled over it in eager delight.

A quick glance convinced him that it was real, and no modern imitation. The wood was sun-dried hickory, worked and polished until it had a surface like stone. Bits of carved bone joined the sections, and the wearing surface was of snakeskin. The antlers were fused in with some sort of resin, reinforced

65

with bone strips and bleached white. And everywhere it was decorated with little bits of colored stone. Over and over in his hands, he turned it, and then took it to the window to examine it more carefully.

Finally he turned to Tony and said, "Tony MacTavish Levy, where did you get this?"

"I took it," Tony answered slowly.

"You mean you stole it?"

"I took it," Tony repeated stubbornly.

"Now where on God's earth could you take a thing like this from?"

"From the guildhall," Tony blurted out, and then the words spilled over each other. "I met Peter Van Doben, and I wanted to go to the Indians but he had to go to the guildhall to pay his father's watch-fee. I went with him and we walked down to the village and to the guildhall. He went in to make the payment of three *thalers*. But I went into the council chamber and there on the big table where the burgomasters sit . . . there it was, because the old sachem left it and took a steel war helmet in return . . . so I took it. I was all alone and no one was watching, so I took it. I don't know why, but I took it. I knew you would want to see it, and I didn't think it would do any harm if I took it and showed it to you and then brought it back. But then they must have discovered it was gone, because the guard-watch began shouting, and I ran out and left Peter. I ran down

along the wall and hid in Hoffman's stable, and then I ran almost all the way to the door. But maybe Peter told them, because two of them came on horses and I ran through the door, and now I can't go back. I can't go back—ever."

And Tony began to cry.

"Sit down," said old Doc Forbes.

So Tony sat down on one of those hard steel chairs that you find in doctors' offices, and went on crying, and old Doc Forbes watched him patiently until he stopped.

"Now," said the doctor, "that is that. I'm not going to ask you again where you got the helm, Tony, because I retain enough of my sanity to know that you couldn't have gotten it in any more reasonable way than you told me. I'm not going to go into the ethics of returning something to people who stopped existing a number of centuries ago. Suppose the two of us take a little trip uptown and call on my friend Ike."

Old Doc Forbes' very quick decision was born more out of desperation than consideration. At that moment, he did not trust his own thoughts sufficiently to have any real desire to remain in their company. He wanted a hard and gimletlike pair of eyes to consider the headdress and to render an opinion on it, and he knew of no colder, more objective gaze, when it came to things Indian, than that of Ike Gilman.

"By the way," he said to Tony, "have you ever been to the Museum of the American Indian?"

Tony shook his head.

"No? Well, we're going there now."

And then old Doc Forbes got an armful of tissue paper, wrapped the headdress shapelessly but carefully, pulled on a black-turning-green coat, mounted his bowler hat on his bald head, and led the way outside.

When Tony understood that he was going for a ride in old Doc Forbes' Model T Ford, his fears dried up along with his tears. This was a fine and special treat, for he had rarely ridden in an automobile before. Especially in such an elegant automobile as this Model T which, old though it was, gave him the same feeling of intimate fellowship combined with dignity as did old Doc Forbes himself. The Model T was a car which might be described as a little bit of an open car and a little bit of a closed car, and old Doc Forbes liked it because it reminded him of the days when he drove a horse and buggy. It was as high as a hansom cab, and on each side it had a fine brass-mounted lamp for driving at night.

And whenever old Doc Forbes threw a handful of sand into the gear box, it was much more like feeding a horse than any filling tank ration of gasoline could be.

Now Tony sat down inside, while old Doc Forbes cranked the motor. He had a fine style of cranking, but when he finally got the motor going and raced for his seat in the car, he always managed to drop his bowler hat. His dash back to get it, and then back to the driver's seat was usually two or three seconds short, so that he would sit down behind a motor which coughed gently and apologetically into silence.

In a small way, this was a fascinating drama, which Tony observed with heightened pleasure, and he nodded his head sagely when Old Doc Forbes observed,

"Someday, Tony, I will leave my hat here while I crank the car. But at that point, I will not be a very good doctor. Do you follow me?"

Tony nodded, and old Doc Forbes was so pleased that he vowed to himself that he would suffer all the pains of an unsatisfied curiosity rather than ask Tony again where the headdress came from. Also, in back of the doctor's mind, there was a suspicion that no matter how much and how earnestly he questioned the boy, the answer would be no different. If it had been anything else in the world other than this particular headdress, the doctor might have suspected a theft. But here was Tony with the one article in the entire United States of America which no one could possibly steal, because it didn't exist to be stolen.

But this kind of thinking made his mind go around and around in a way that was particularly unhealthy for a family physician. Finally old Doc Forbes gave it up and set himself to share Tony's enjoyment of the ride.

And Tony was enjoying the ride. Since he had rarely taken an automobile ride before, this one was satisfactory in every possible way. A ride on a circus elephant would not have been better than their progress along Houston Street, and then up Sixth Avenue, under the noisy Sixth Avenue elevated tracks.

They drove through a Central Park all pale green and lovely yellow in its springtime bloom, and old Doc Forbes asked, somewhat lightly, "Not so different, is it, Tony, from how it looks when you go through the door?"

Tony smiled and nodded; for how could he explain to anyone the lush fairyland that Manhattan Island had once been, with which not even Central Park as it was today could compare?

Across One Hundred and Tenth Street, they drove to Riverside Drive, and up along the Hudson River, so broad and beautiful and sparkling all over with such pleasant sunshine. Past Grant's Tomb they drove, with the Model T coughing only modestly and performing nobly, and then over to Broadway and One Hundred and Fifty-fifth Street, where Tony gazed in unconcealed delight at the handsome clump of buildings and the fine open plaza.

"There it is," said old Doc Forbes, as he worked the Model T into a parking space, "and now you and I are going to beard the old lion in his den. And if Ike Gilman should show human qualities, don't be taken in, Tony, my boy. Let me do the talking, and when it comes to your part, follow my lead."

He got out of the car and cocked his head at Tony, and then added, as an afterthought, "About that door—I wouldn't mention it, if I were you, Tony. You understand and I understand, but Ike Gilman . . ."

"I won't," said Tony. Then they shook hands, and old Doc Forbes winked at Tony and even danced a few steps of an old-fashioned jig.

"Tony," he said, "you may not realize it, but this is shaping up as the greatest day of my life."

They were sitting in the curator's office, and Tony's head was teeming with the things he had seen on the way in. He had never dreamed that a museum could be a wonderful place like this, every step an adventure. Some day soon, he would come back here if they would let him, and spend hours wandering around and looking at everything. A hint of a thought, of a totally new idea, was beginning to come to him. It occurred to him that perhaps there was more than one magic door.

But he hardly had time to think about that now. He sat in a big chair in the big, sunny office of the curator. The office was crowded with things that had not yet gone to the shelves and not yet gone to the basement, but were rather in a state of suspended animation between the two. There were feather war bonnets and great bows and drums and war clubs and buckskin moccasins and little birchbark canoes and belts of wampum and tomahawks and ceremonial pipes. But none of these treasures appeared to impress old Doc Forbes, who sat with great self-satisfaction, the tissue-wrapped headdress cradled tenderly in his lap.

He had introduced Tony very simply and directly, telling the tall, skinny, long-limbed, long-faced man, "This is my friend and associate, Tony MacTavish Levy."

Ike Gilman blinked his pale blue eyes once or twice, nodded, and shook hands gravely. In some ways, he reminded Tony of the doctor; in other ways, he did not. But he put Tony at ease. After his first moment of fear, Tony was not uncomfortable with him again.

"Well," said Ike Gilman, after the introductions were over, "is the medical profession—or your own brand of quackery —so sparse that you can afford to waste my afternoons as well as my evenings?"

"Better to waste them with me than waste them alone in this morgue," answered old Doc Forbes.

"This morgue, as you call it," said the curator, "contains the treasures of a lost era and a great people."

"Bah!"

"What?"

"Bah!" said old Doc Forbes. "Bah! Don't you know what *bah* means? It's an expression of contempt."

"What are you driving at, you old goat?"

"Treasures!" said old Doc Forbes. "What kind of treasures have you got here? A moth-eaten collection of useless relics that are not even unique. Bows, arrows, war clubs, wampum! Any little western tourist museum can boast the same thing."

"And they allow a child to be in your company!" Turning to Tony, the curator said, "Your associate, if I may say so, Tony, is a man of little wisdom and less grace."

"Grace," snorted old Doc Forbes.

"What are you hiding in that tissue paper?" asked Ike Gilman.

"Nothing of any consequence. Just a little trinket my associate and I are working with."

"Just happened to bring it with you, huh?" squinted the curator.

"Just happened that way."

"You old goat! I know you like a book—trying to disarm me by bringing a child along—lull me into trustfulness and then try to palm off some cheap, fake medicine-show war bonnet as Sitting Bull's own! Well, it won't work. Take it back to the auction room where you got it."

"War bonnet? Good heavens," said old Doc Forbes innocently. "You don't think I came here to sell you something?"

"I never knew you to give me anything."

"Perhaps we ought to go, Tony," said old Doc Forbes plaintively. "My friend, Mr. Gilman, is much too cynical."

Tony, who had been puzzled and somewhat abashed by this fierce exchange, started to rise, but the curator waved him back to his chair, directed a long, bony finger at the doctor, and roared, "What have you got in that tissue paper?"

"Nothing. Nothing at all." And old Doc Forbes unwrapped the headdress and placed it on the curator's desk. "Nothing at all."

What amazed Tony was that the curator's reaction should have been so like the doctor's. At first he tried to speak, but the words wouldn't come out. Then he gave up trying to speak and bent over his desk, staring at the headdress, and giving Tony the impression that in another moment his eyes would pop out. Then he touched the headdress gently. He picked it up, turned it over, and examined it with intense interest. Then he abandoned forty years of pedagogical dignity, dashed to the door of his office, and woke the sedate spaces of the museum as they had never been wakened before.

"Atkins!" he roared. "Miss Morrison! Goldstein!"

In a few minutes, every member of the museum staff was in his office, crowding around the headdress. And old Doc Forbes, sitting comfortably in his chair, winked at Tony.

An hour later, old Doc Forbes was just as placid and just as undisturbed, and he smiled beneficently upon Ike Gilman, who was shouting at him, "You're not a doctor! You're not a scientist! You're a highwayman!"

"Take it or leave it," said old Doc Forbes gently. "The price is seven hundred and fifty dollars and not one penny less. Take it or leave it."

"But I tell you the purchase fund cannot spare seven hundred and fifty dollars!"

"Was there ever a purchase fund that could? And here I've priced it so cheaply that I should actually examine my conscience and ask myself whether or not, out of friendship for you, I'm not cheating my associate, Tony MacTavish Levy. Well, perhaps we're wasting your time and ours. There are other museums. There's Natural History. There's the Smithsonian. I can do business with a private collector, or maybe I can even afford it myself. Be kind of nice to own the only bonnet of that kind in the world. As a matter of fact, I kind of cotton to the idea. Friendship, after all, has its limitations."

"Friendship!" snorted the curator.

"Come along, Tony," said old Doc Forbes.

"Wait a minute!" cried the curator, picking up the headdress and fondling it and examining it again. "It would be just like you to give it to Johnson at Natural History. After all, you old buzzard, I've known you half a century. Be reasonable. At least you owe it to me to tell me where this came from."

"As I said, from my associate, Tony MacTavish Levy."

"As you said! How do I know it's not a fake?"

"That's why they pay you a salary," said old Doc Forbes comfortably. "When a man's sick, I know it. If you don't know if that's a genuine crown of a Great Lord of the Iroquois Confederation, then you're a fake."

Ignoring this, the curator turned on Tony and demanded, "Now where did this come from, son?"

"I can't tell you, sir," answered Tony.

"You mean you don't know?"

"He means that I advised him not to tell, and just what are you going to do about it?" asked old Doc Forbes sweetly.

"How do I know it's not stolen?"

"From where?" inquired old Doc Forbes, with ultimate logic. "If one of them existed anywhere in America, you would know about it. And if it doesn't exist, it can't be stolen, can it?"

"But it does exist!" shouted the curator.

"Precisely," smiled old Doc Forbes.

"It exists! Here it is!" shouted the curator, picking it up.

"The logic is admirable, but I have my patients and Tony has his home to go to; so we'll both have to be running along."

"Five hundred," begged the curator.

"Ike," said old Doc Forbes gravely, "seven hundred and fifty is the price. Not a penny more, not a penny less. Take it or leave it."

"All right, you bandit," muttered the curator. "You win. But now it's mine. Don't lay a hand on it."

"And make out the check to Tony MacTavish Levy," said old Doc Forbes, smiling sweetly . . .

They were in the Model T again and driving downtown, when the doctor said to Tony, looking straight ahead of him, "Only one thing, son. You and I have become associates, in a way, and an association is no darn good if the partners can't tell each other the truth. I want to know if you stole that helm. Not from someone who's been dead these three hundred years —but from someone alive and kicking today. Did you or didn't you, Tony?"

"I didn't," said Tony.

"All right. That's enough for me, and maybe someday you'll tell me more about it. I won't press you. But now that we're operating in high finance, so as to speak, things are a little complicated. I guess I'll drive home with you and have a talk with your mother and father."

"I would appreciate that a great deal," answered Tony. "Also," he said with more difficulty, "I want to tell you, Dr. Forbes, that you are the best friend I guess I ever had. I don't know how to thank you."

"Don't thank me," grinned the doctor. "More fun than I ever had in my life. But you know something, Tony, I got a funny notion you won't be going through that door any more."

Strangely enough, Tony was thinking much the same way. Yet there were other doors he knew he would be going through —the door to Ike Gilman's museum to begin with.